WORMWAR

PART 1

WRITTEN BY **FRANK FORTE**
ILLUSTRATED BY **SZYMON KUDRANSKI**

WORMS.

THERE ARE MANY TYPES.

SOME ARE *HARMLESS* AND HAVE THEIR PLACE IN NATURE.

OTHERS CAN BE *NASTY PARASITES* THAT SUCK THE LIFE OUT OF ANYTHING THEY BITE INTO.

TAKE, FOR INSTANCE, *THE HOOKWORM*. ITS *INSIDIOUS* CYCLE OF LIFE HAS BEEN *PROPAGATING* SINCE THE DAWN OF TIME. THEIR LARVAE SIT ON THE GROUND AND WAIT FOR AN UNAWARE VICTIM TO STEP ON THEM. THE BASTARDS EASILY *PENETRATE* THE EXPOSED SKIN AND ARE CARRIED BY THE BLOOD TO THE *INTESTINE* OR *LUNGS*.

ONCE INSIDE THE LARVAE ATTACHES ITSELF TO IT'S NEW HOST WITH ITS *HOOKS*. IT MAKES ITSELF COMFORTABLE AND *FEEDS* OFF THE *BLOOD*.

THE FEMALE PRODUCES 30,000 EGGS PER DAY THAT ARE PASSED FROM THE INTESTINE WITH THE FECES.

THIS FURTHER CONTAMINATES THE SOIL AND WATER AND THE *INFECTION* OF *INNOCENT CREATURES* CONTINUES.

SO MUCH LIKE THE *PROLIFERATION* OF *CRIME* IN PITTSBURGH. IT'S A *DISEASE* THAT CAN'T SEEM TO BE STOPPED.

DECADES AGO YOU WOULD JAIL A CRIMINAL AND HE'D BE OFF THE STREETS. NOWADAYS HE'S OUT IN A FEW HOURS THANKS TO A SLICK LAWYER. TIMES HAVE *CHANGED*.

AND SO HAVE THE *CRIMES*.

MILITARY WEAPONRY AND *BIOTECHNOLOGY* HAVE SEEPED INTO THE UNDERGROUND LIKE *ACID RAIN*.

ONE OF THE GROUPS THAT HAS INCORPORATED *BIOTECH* INTO THEIR CRIME WAVES GOES BY THE NAME OF *NECROWORM*. A SECRET SYNDICATE HEADED UP BY A GROUP OF *RENEGADE BIO-SCIENTISTS*.

INFO ON THEM IS SCARCE, BUT THANKS TO A THUG I ROUGHED UP, I GOT SOME INTEL THAT LED ME *HERE*. LOOKS LIKE MY CITY HAS *WORMS*.

AND IT'S GOING TO TAKE MORE THAN *A PILL* TO CURE IT.

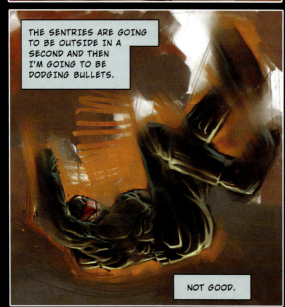

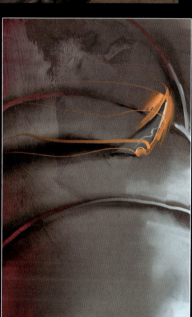

WARLASH THE DEMON

WRITTEN BY **FRANK FORTE** ART BY **MARCIN PONOMAREW** COLORS BY **MARCIN PONOMAREW** AND **FRANK FORTE**

WILKINSBURG. PARTS OF IT ARE NICE; PARTS OF IT ARE NOT.

THE PART I'M IN IS KNOWN FOR CRIME ACTVITY.

I INTERCEPTED A CALL ON THE POLICE SCANNER. SOMEHOW AN HYSTERICAL WOMAN GOT THROUGH. SHE WAS COMPLAINING OF SCREAMING COMING FROM A BUILDING AT 3477 PITT ST.

I ASSUME THE COPS WON'T COME HERE...AND I'M RIGHT.

NO ONE IN SIGHT.

DOOR'S OPEN

BEFORE I ENTER THE BUILDING, I SMELL *FRESH BLOOD*. THAT USUALLY LEADS TO A CARCAS OR TWO. AND SURE ENOUGH I'M *DEAD ON*.

THERE ARE BODIES ALL OVER THE PLACE. LOOKS LIKE THEY'VE BEEN *RIPPED APART*.

A PENTAGRAM IS DRAWN IN THE CENTER OF THE FLOOR. MY GUESS IS THAT A BUNCH OF *METH HEADS* WATCHED TOO MANY *HORROR MOVIES* AND WANTED TO *PLAY WITH SATAN*.

IF THE DEVIL DOES EXIST, HE'D SURE BE PROUD OF THIS MESS.

THESE MURDERS ARE THE WORK OF A *MADMAN!*

AND WHOEVER *IS* RESPONSIBLE WILL HAVE TO ANSWER TO ME.

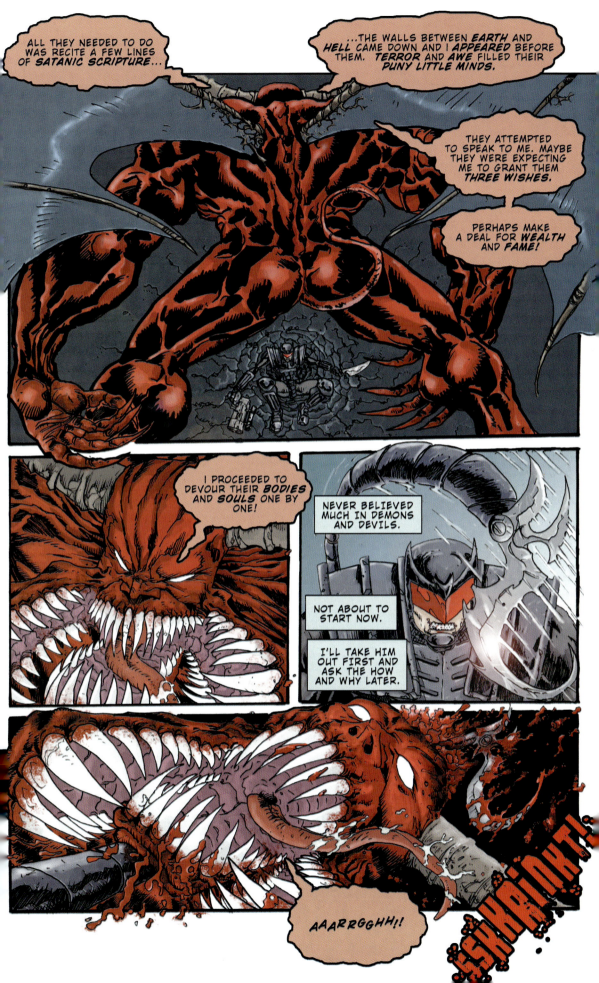

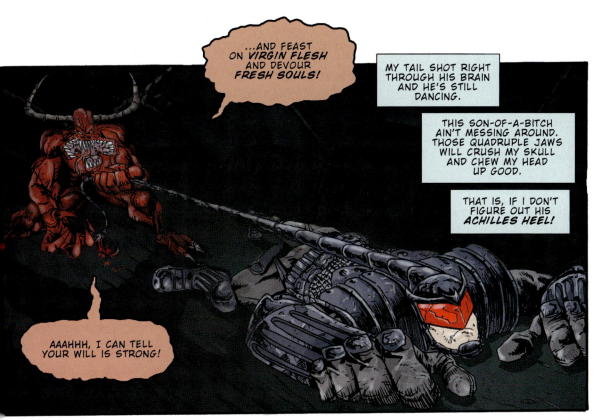

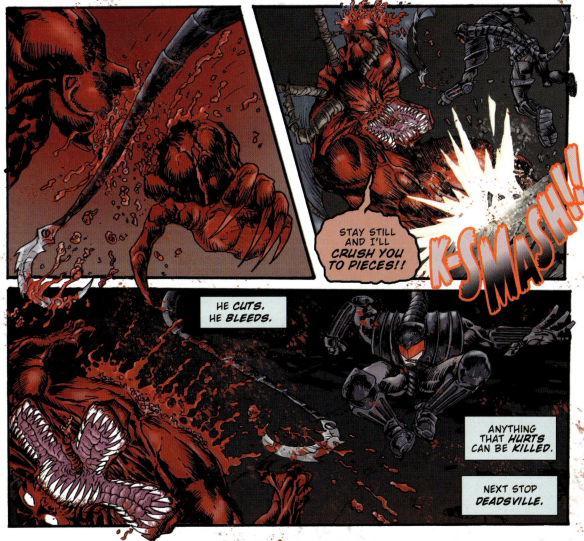

TO BE CONTINUED...

ASYLUM PRESS

WARLASH

ZOMBIE MUTANT GENESIS

96 PAGE TRADE PAPERBACK ONE-SHOT!

"...a rollercoaster ride over razor blades!"
--Robert S. Rhine
(Girls and Corpses)

SPECIAL PREVIEW #0 ON SALE NOW!

PULSE POUNDING NEO NOIR FICTION IN THE SENSATIONAL RAW CARNAGE STYLE

PART 1 IN THE ZOMBIE MUTANT MASSACRE TRILOGY!

written by FRANK FORTE art by ALEKSANDAR SOTIROVSKI and FRANK FORTE cover by BEN OLSON

A BIO-GENESIS OF TERROR!
VIEW TRAILER and PREVIEW ONLINE
warlash.com

WARLASH is © and a registered TM of Frank Forte 2007. Visit www.asylumpress.com for more info.

WARLASH

ASYLUM PRESS

ZOMBIE MUTANT MEGAWAR

written by FRANK FORTE and ERIC ROCHFORD   illustrated by FRANK FORTE   cover by BEN OLSON

96 PAGE TRADE PAPERBACK ONE-SHOT!

PART 2 IN THE ZOMBIE MUTANT MASSACRE TRILOGY!

VIEW TRAILER and PREVIEW ONLINE
WARLASH.COM

ASYLUM PRESS MAIL ORDER
For more goodies visit: www.ASYLUMPRESS.com

WARLASH ZOMBIE MUTANT GENESIS TPB - $5

WARLASH No. 0 ZOMBIE MUTANT GENESIS SPECIAL EDITION - $3

WARLASH : DARK NOIR No. 1 - $4

UNDEAD EVIL TPB - $5

UNDEAD EVIL No. 0 SPECIAL EDITION - $3

ASYLUM OF HORRORS No. 1 - $5 GIANT-SIZED 88 PGS

BILLY BOY # 1 - $3

BILLY BOY # 2 - $3

CLETUS AND FLOYD # 1 - $3

Deadly Are The Naked REGULAR - $10

CHESTACLESE SKETCHBOOK No. 1 - $7

DTOX No. 0 SPECIAL EDITION - $3

SATAN'S CIRCUS OF HELL TPB - $20

SATAN'S POWDER ROOM # 1 - $3

CHICKEN SOUP FOR SATAN # 1 - $3

SATAN GONE WILD # 1 - $3

HEX OF THE WICKED WITCH TPB - COMING SOON GIANT-SIZED 128 PGS

THE BOMB TPB - $15 by STEVE MANNION GIANT-SIZED 176 PGS

SHIPPING & HANDLING: $2 FOR 1-10 BOOKS
$3 FOR 11-20 BOOKS
CANADIAN ORDERS ADD $5
FOREIGN ORDERS ADD $10 (AIR SHIPPED)
PayPal PAY PAL AVAILABLE ONLINE

SEND CHECK OR MONEY ORDER TO:
ASYLUM PRESS PO BOX 2875 HOLLYWOOD CA 90078 USA

MORE BACK ISSUES ONLINE!

INSIDIOUS TALES # 1 - $3

FROM BEYONDE # 1 - $5

FROM BEYONDE # 2 - $5

FROM BEYONDE # 3 - $5

COMPLETE VAMPIRE VERSES SET AVAILABLE ONLINE

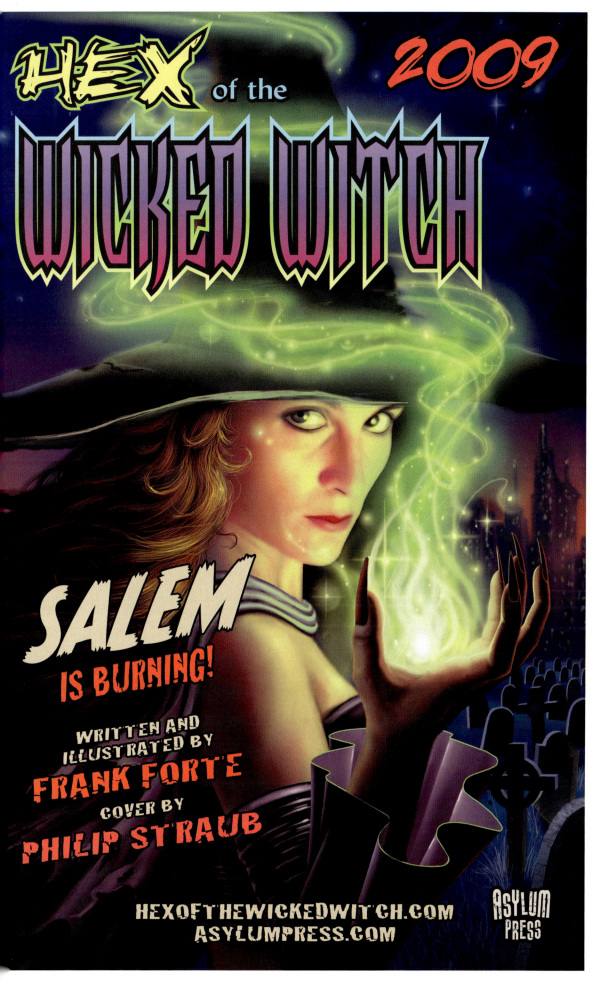